Judith Byron Schachner

YO, VIKINGS!

DUTTON CHILDREN'S BOOKS

New York

Published in the United States 2002 by Dutton Children's Books,

a division of Penguin Putnam Books for Young Readers

345 Hudson Street, New York, New York 10014

www.penguinputnam.com

Designed by Heather Wood

Printed in China

First Edition

ISBN 0-525-46889-7

1   3   5   7   9   10   8   6   4   2

In memory of Poppy

—J.B.S.

On Halloween and every day in between, Emma was a furry red fox with a thick bushy tail. It was no game. She really believed it.

But this fox could draw. Her journals were full of characters, ranging from raptors to Robin Hoods to ring-tailed lemurs. Emma had been all of them at one point or another. And no one knew what Emma would become next.

At school, Emma's class was planning for World Discovery Day, and each student had to prepare a speech about a famous explorer of the past.

"I'm Christopher Columbus," shouted Nikki Tibbles after he pulled his name out of Mrs. Mukherjee's hat. Emma's friend Zinzi was thrilled to be Sacajawea.

Emma was the last to draw. She waited a moment, then said, "I'm Erik the Red . . . Fox."

"Who's Erik the Red Fox?" asked Murphy Bean.

"I don't know," said Emma. "But I sure do like the sound of his name."

That afternoon, Emma took her brother, Ollie, to the library. Mr. Sigurd, the librarian, stood tall as an oak tree behind his old desk.

"I'm searching for Erik the Red," said Emma. "He's an explorer."

"Viking," said Mr. Sigurd in a deep and solemn voice. The children followed him until he stopped and pointed to a row of Very Old Books.

"Here lies the story of Erik the Red," he said, then turned to Ollie and warned, "Beware of the Jotuns." In the blink of an eye, Mr. Sigurd was gone.

"What show tunes?" asked Ollie.

Emma sat down with her big pile of books right there in the stacks. Ollie stuck his thumb in his mouth and cuddled up next to her. A moment later he was asleep. Emma was spellbound as she read about the seafaring people who discovered America five hundred years before Christopher Columbus. She marveled at their magical sailing ships decorated with the snarling heads and swirling tails of dragons. Emma opened her journal and began to draw a beautiful boat full of foxes sailing to Valhalla, the Viking Hall of Fallen Heroes.

At home, Emma grabbed tinfoil and glue. She quickly smushed twelve sheets of tinfoil into the shape of a helmet just like the ones she saw in the books. She tossed a velvet skirt over her shoulders and raided her mom's jewelry box for a sparkly brooch to pin to her cape.

After she had cut her sword and shield from cardboard, Emma unpinned her glorious fox tail and carefully glued it all around her helmet. That's the moment Emma the Red Fox became Emma the Red, Viking Explorer.

The next morning, a fierce-looking Viking handed Ollie a stone with a picture painted on it.

"It's a rune," said Emma as she grabbed her lunch and galloped out the door to school.

"Emma wants a Biking ship for her birthday," warned Ollie, pointing to the picture on the stone. "You can buy it at the Biking store."

Emma spent every day after school at the library plundering the shelves for more Viking books, but Mr. Sigurd was the biggest help of all. His old noggin was so full of Viking facts and fables that Emma made him an honorary Viking.

"We shall call you Sigurd the Smart," she said, and placed a tinfoil helmet she had made for him on his snowy white head.

On World Discovery Day, Emma was the best-prepared explorer of all.

But nothing prepared her for the surprise Mr. Sigurd had waiting for her at the library after school that day. He smiled as he handed Emma an ad from the city newspaper.

Emma's eyes grew as round as jelly doughnuts when she read the words "Viking Ship for Sale."

Now, some might say it was pure coincidence that there was a Viking ship for sale in the newspaper. But Emma the Red believed it was the mighty Viking god Odin himself who had placed it there just for her.

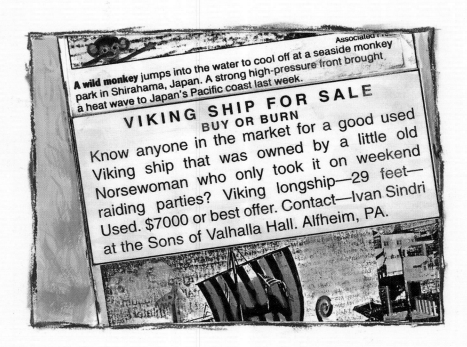

A wild monkey jumps into the water to cool off at a seaside monkey park in Shirahama, Japan. A strong high-pressure front brought a heat wave to Japan's Pacific coast last week.

VIKING SHIP FOR SALE
BUY OR BURN
Know anyone in the market for a good used Viking ship that was owned by a little old Norsewoman who only took it on weekend raiding parties? Viking longship—29 feet— Used. $7000 or best offer. Contact—Ivan Sindri at the Sons of Valhalla Hall. Alfheim, PA.

Emma begged and pleaded with her parents, but she knew they just didn't have $7000 for a ship, so she came up with a plan.

"Bring me your piggy bank," Emma commanded Ollie, "and I'll go get mine." Together they counted their change on her bedroom floor.

"Now we have to write an important letter," she said. "We have to make the Viking man the very best offer, just like it said in the paper."

"The bestest!" added Ollie.

All Emma could think about was the Viking ship. She told Ollie story after story and drew their adventures in her journal.

"Odin is riding his eight-legged horse, and I'm sailing alongside in my beautiful new Viking ship," began Emma.

"What about me?" asked Ollie.

"We are being chased by the horrible Jotuns," continued Emma, ignoring her brother. "The Jotuns are gaining speed—closer and closer they come. Now we can see their ugly stone heads and feel the chill of their giant icy feet. But just as the Jotuns are about to crush us, Thor's hammer thunders down through the clouds and . . ."

"Suppertime!" called their mom.

Talk about Emma getting a Viking ship spread across the school-yard like butter on hot toast. It had been a whole week without a response from Mr. Sindri, but that didn't keep Emma from telling everyone that she was getting a Viking ship for her birthday. It was the perfect present.

"I don't believe her," said Nikki Tibbles.

"Why would she make it up?" said Zinzi.

"Because," answered Murphy Bean, "Emma makes everything up."

It didn't matter that most of the kids called Emma's story "Viking voodoo." She still believed. And she knew that Mr. Sigurd, the librarian, believed too.

When she and Ollie arrived for story hour, Mr. Sigurd was enchanting his young audience with the tale of a dragon slayer who burned his thumb while cooking the heart of the dragon Fafnir.

Most of the children laughed, but Emma believed every word.

At bedtime, when Emma and Ollie were cozy in their jammies, the little Viking continued the story as she drew. "Suddenly, Nidhogg the Bearded Dragon challenges Sigurd the Smart for Fafnir's half-eaten heart. *Chomp, chomp, chomp,* goes the dragon.

"Save your life, Sigurd!" shouted Emma. "Listen to the wisdom of the birds."

"Yeah," shouted Ollie. "Wisten to the boods."

By Emma's birthday, there was still no word from Mr. Sindri, and the only Viking ship sighted was the one painted in frosting on her delicious cake. When Nikki Tibbles and Murphy Bean walked through the gate, they scoped out the yard.

"So, Emma, where's the giant ship?" they teased. Emma's eyes filled with tears, and she ran into the house. Ollie came running after her.

"I told them the show tunes would get them," he said, thrusting his wobbly sword into the air. Emma couldn't help but laugh. She hugged her little brother, then bravely walked back outside to have fun at her party. At the end, Emma blew out her candles and made one last wish. Odin must have been listening, because soon Ollie appeared, bearing an opened letter.

"Weed it," he said.

So Emma did, and then she let out a whoop and a holler that could be heard all the way to Gimle. "The Viking ship is coming tomorrow!"

At 6:30, a large crowd had gathered in front of Emma's house. By 7:00, a TV news van had pulled up with a camera crew and a reporter. Emma saw her entire class rounding the corner, all dressed as Vikings. Even Mrs. Mukherjee was in costume.

"Quick, get a shot of the kids," directed the reporter. The cameraman spun around just as a burly truck driver shouted, "Yo, Vikings straight ahead!"

Then Emma saw it, and Ollie saw it too. It was not a drawing or some crazy adventure made up in Emma's head. The ship was as

real as her friends and oh so beautiful, silhouetted against the last blaze of twilight.

The manly men, dressed as Vikings, hauled the hulking ship into Emma's yard. They sang:

"Now give me bread,
Now give me drink,
Or it's down to the depths I fear,
To Niflheim I sink!
YO-wee-O! YO-wee-O! YO-wee-O! YO-wee-O!"

It took a while for the Viking men to settle the ship onto its wooden cradle, which Emma's dad and his friend Harvey had made in the backyard. But once finished, Emma and Ollie were the first to

board. Emma dropped sail while Ollie hugged the neck of the dragon. In minutes they were joined by Mrs. Mukherjee and the whole class. Even Nikki Tibbles, the nonbeliever, climbed aboard.

"Hoy! Wait for me!" called a voice from below. At first Emma hardly recognized the man in the cloak and tunic, but then she saw that it was Mr. Sigurd.

"Have any room for an old librarian?" he bellowed up to the crew.

"There shall always be room for Sigurd the Smart," shouted back Emma.

"But where's your sword?" asked Ollie.

"Spare the sword, summon a book," declared the librarian. "Words can calm even the Mightiest of Beasts. And you never know when there will be a lull in the adventure."

Now that everyone had boarded, Emma opened her journal and began to draw her beautiful ship rolling high on the waves, past dragons dreaming of books, past beast and bear, and beyond the shimmering frozen fjords where Leif the Lucky and his aged father, Erik the Red, fish for Odin's golden amulets.

"See, Ollie," said Emma, looking into her little brother's eyes. "Dreams do come true."

"Yup," said Ollie. "And not just for Bikings."

Author's Note

"God deliver us from the fury of the Northmen." These words were offered in prayer by those who lived along the shores of northwestern Europe during the Vikings' reign of terror. These sea-roaming thieves in their longships with the bloodred sails raided and ransacked towns up and down the coast and inland from the eighth to the eleventh centuries. The word *Viking* comes from the Norse language, in which to go "a-viking" meant to sail off, to go adventuring.

But the Vikings were much more than pillagers and plunderers. Originating in Norway, Sweden, and Denmark, the Northmen were advanced shipbuilders, superb sailors, and fearless explorers. They were clever at trading and talented at crafting, and they enjoyed a rich storytelling culture. Known for the carvings of ferocious beasts on the prows of their slender sailing ships, they navigated their vessels through dangerous, uncharted waters and later colonized the nearby lands. Sailing west, they discovered and settled the habitable places between Scandinavia and North America—all within two centuries.

By A.D. 985 an Icelandic chieftain with a fiery temper founded two settlements on an island in the North Atlantic, mostly covered in ice and snow. His name was Erik the Red, and he was very clever at marketing, for he called this new island "Greenland." When his countrymen heard of this beautiful place, they soon followed in fourteen ships bearing all kinds of animals, including dogs and cats.

Erik the Red's son, Leif (also known as Leif Eriksson or Leif the Lucky), grew up to be an explorer as well. In the year 1000, he became the first European to set foot on North American shores. Yes, Leif landed first, nearly five hundred years before Christopher Columbus. He stayed through the winter, then returned home to Greenland with a cargo of timber and wild grapes. The Vikings called this good land "Vinland."

Some believe that Leif the Lucky voyaged as far south as Cape Cod, with its warm tides and *Furdustrandir* (heavenly strands of beaches). This is a place where my family has spent many summers exploring, building castles, and sculpting dragons in the hot sand that may have once warmed the toes of the Vikings.

On behalf of my own two little Vikings—my daughters, Emma and Sarah—I wish to thank Mr. Ivar Christensen, the Leif Eriksson Society International, Mr. Gene Martenson, and the men of the Leif Eriksson Viking Ship Inc. They provided a boat full of fun and learning for many children.

In 1964 the U.S. Congress passed a bill designating October 9 as Leif Eriksson Day. For many years, Sue Larson, a teacher in Swarthmore, Pennsylvania, and her third-grade class celebrated this day on the Viking ship in my backyard, which belonged to Emma and Sarah. There the children learned that Leif landed in North America before Columbus. Then they learned just how much fun it was to go "a-viking."

If you want to read more about the Vikings, here are some books you might enjoy:

Almgren, Bertil, and others. *The Viking*. New York: Crescent Books, a division of Random House, Inc., 1975.

D'Aulaire, Inge, and Edgar D'Aulaire. *Norse Gods and Giants*. Garden City, N.Y.: Doubleday & Co., Inc., 1967.

Johasson, Bjorn, trans. *The Sayings of the Vikings*. (Translated from the original Icelandic.) Reykjavík, Iceland: Gudrun Publishing House, 1992.

Margeson, Susan, and Peter Anderson, photographer. *The Vikings* (An Eyewitness Book). New York: Alfred A. Knopf, Inc., 1992.

Nicholson, Robert, and Claire Watts. *The Vikings: Facts, Stories and Activities*. New York: Scholastic, Inc., 1991.